We Like Snow!

by Miriam Sklar

ISBN: 978-1-338-75085-0
Illustrated by John Lund

Published by Scholastic Inc., 557 Broadway, New York, NY 10012

10 9 8 7 6 5 4 68 25 26 27/0

Printed in Jiaxing, China. First printing, January 2021.

We like snow.

We like snowflakes.

We like snow forts.

We like snowballs.

We like snowmen.

We like snow angels.

We like snow!